the
ABCs
of
RPGs

By Ivan Van Norman
Illustrated by Caleb Cleveland

A is for Adventure

may you always be on one!

B is for
Book

the source of all our fun!

C is for Creatures

of every shape and size

D is for Dice

can you count all the sides?

E is for *Enchantment*,
do you like Jump, Light, or Blessed?

F is for *Friendship*,
the ones we make
on quests!

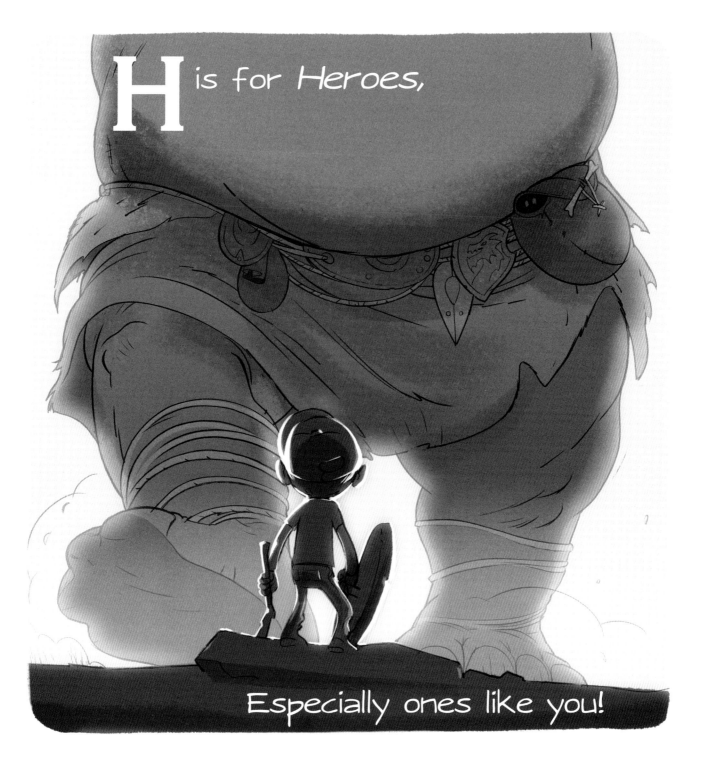

I is for Imagination

what is YOUR favorite tale?

J is for Journey

let's wander
down the trail

L is for *Lost,*
which is sometimes just as fun!

M is for *Mystery,* it starts from this small seed

N

is for *Nature,* which is something we all need

O is for Owlbear,

this one's name is Chris!

P is for Planning,

so 'How do you want to do this?'

Q is for Questing,

It's time to pack our bags.

R is for Ruins!

...Where history gets to brag

S is for *Ship,*

they will keep you off your feet

T is for Treasure,

because getting stuff is sweet!

...full of risk, and often cold!

V is for Villains,

either cowardly or bold

W is for Wisdom,

unlock the knowledge from within

Z is for Zeal,

...How our heroes saved the day!

OUR AUTHORS

"To my little boy Phoenix, and my best friend - His mother. May you both forever shine and have many adventures in your life" - Ivan

"To my wife Karen and my daughters Eleanor and Leura, for always reminding me to see life's adventures as would a kid."- CC

Author: Ivan Van Norman
Art: Caleb Cleveland
Layout: Christopher J. De La Rosa

Printed in China
First Printing
1 2 3 4 5 6 7 8 9 10

ISBN: 978-0-9976711-0-0
Library of Congress Control Number: 2016909244

Visit our website at huntersbooks.com to learn more about the *ABCs of RPGs* and download the sing-along-song by *The Library Bards!*

Thank you to all our Kickstarter Backers, without you, this would not exist!